Farmer Ham

Written by
Alec Sillifant

Illustrated by
Mike Spoor

meadowside

The crows were happy,
and they were happy because, as usual,
they were in Farmer Ham's cornfield eating corn.

All day long they would sit in the cornfield, singing, dancing and stuffing themselves with Farmer Ham's corn.

Day after day, Farmer Ham would run out of his farmhouse waving his arms and shouting as loud as he could to try and get rid of the crows, but the crows would just fly up into the air shouting,

"Silly old

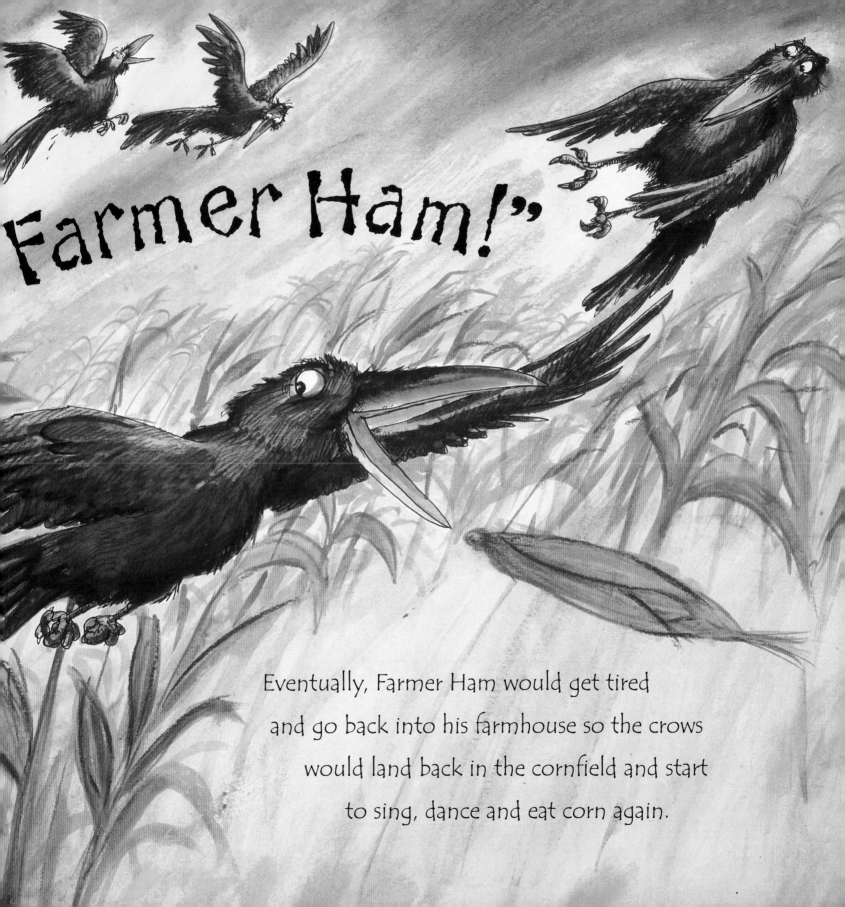

Farmer Ham!"

Eventually, Farmer Ham would get tired
and go back into his farmhouse so the crows
would land back in the cornfield and start
to sing, dance and eat corn again.

Then one day Farmer Ham came out of his farmhouse, but didn't run and shout at all.

He walked up the path from the farmhouse, past the gate to the cornfield, past his old tractor and straight past the crows until he came to the pond at the edge of the cornfield.

"That's funny," said one crow.
"That's not funny," said another.

"This is funny!"
(and he pulled a face.) All the
crows started laughing and shouting,

"silly old Farmer Ham!"

At the pond, Farmer Ham sat down,
took out a fishing rod and began to fish.

"There are no fish in that pond," said one of the crows.

"He's not wearing a coat," said another.

"Maybe he wants to catch a cold instead of fish?"

All the crows snorted with laughter, shouting,

"Silly old Farmer Ham!"

Farmer Ham carried on fishing and soon
he pulled out a dirty old boot from the pond.

"Hey, Farmer Ham," said one crow.
"You can't make a fish pie from an old boot."

"He could always eat the 'sole'," said
another, and all the crows laughed.

As Farmer Ham walked away, carrying the
dirty old boot, all the crows sniggered, shouting,

"Silly old Farmer Ham!"

The next day, Farmer Ham went back to the pond
and began to fish again. All the crows watched him
until, this time, he pulled out a bent and twisted top hat.

"He's as mad as a hatter!" said one crow.

"He must be soft in the head!" said another.

All the crows laughed as Farmer Ham walked
away with the bent and twisted top hat,
shouting after him,

"silly old Farmer Ham!"

On the third day, Farmer Ham went to the
pond again. He started to fish. This time he
pulled out a long, slime-covered scarf.

"Maybe he thinks it's an eel?" said one crow.

"'e'll soon regret it if he does," said another.

All the crows laughed, shouting,

"Silly old Farmer Ham!"

as he made his way back
to the farmhouse, carrying
the long, slimy scarf.

On the fourth day, Farmer Ham went fishing
in the pond again, and this time pulled out
a tatty jacket and a ripped pair of trousers.

"You'd think he'd have given up by now," said one crow.

"Yeah, he's just not suited to it at all," said another.

All the crows laughed.
In fact, they were laughing so hard they were rolling on the floor with tears in their eyes and it took all their effort to keep on shouting,

"Silly old Farmer Ham!"

While the crows lay on the floor unable to do
anything but laugh, Farmer Ham collected
together all the things he had fished
out from the pond, went into his
barn and closed the door.

When the crows stopped laughing
they looked around quite puzzled.

"Hey, where has Farmer Ham gone?" they said.
"He's not by the pond," said one.
"He's not in the field," said another.
"Maybe he's not," said a third.
"But something is, look!"

The frightened crows disappeared into the distance screaming and shouting that they were never going near that cornfield again. Then Farmer Ham looked at the terrifying figure standing in his cornfield and smiled.

clever old Farmer Ham!

For Tracey, whose patience and inner calm
are boundless... luckily for me.
A.S.

For Imogen.
M.S.

First published in 2004
by Meadowside Children's Books,
185 Fleet Street, London EC4A 2HS

Text ©Alec Sillifant 2004
Illustrations ©Mike Spoor 2004
The rights of Alec Sillifant and Mike Spoor to be
identified as the author and illustrator have
been asserted in accordance with the Copyright,
Designs and Patents Act, 1988

A CIP catalogue record for this book
is available from the British Library
10 9 8 7 6 5 4 3 2 1
Printed in U.A.E.